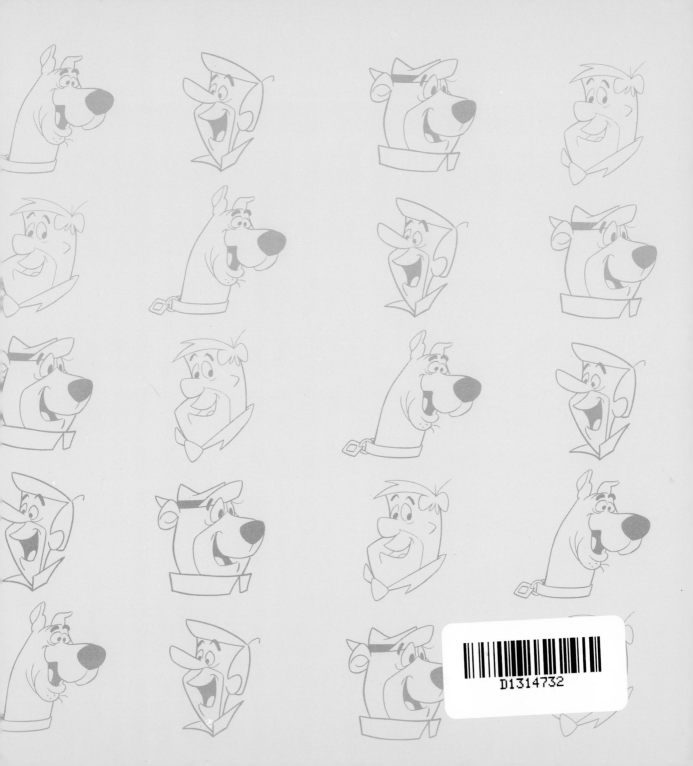

A GAGGLE OF GALLOPING GHOSTS

story adapted by Dandi Mackall and Scott Awley
pencils by Iwao Takamoto
color illustrations by Darryl Goudreau

It was a dark, cloudy night as Scooby-Doo and the gang drove their Mystery Machine toward a spooky looking castle!

"Look, gang! There's Franken Castle!" Freddy shouted as the van wound up the hill. "It's the only castle imported from Transylvania!"

"I can hardly wait to see it," said Velma.

"Well, *I* can wait!" exclaimed Daphne. "Haven't you heard all those werewolf stories?"

Shaggy and Scooby exchanged a frightened look. "Werewolfs? Gulp!"

When they passed a gypsy wagon, the gang decided to get their fortunes told!

"Gather round, my pretties," said Carlotta the gypsy. She started with an incantation! "Spirits rise and spirits fall. Reveal your secrets, tell us all!" Suddenly, the crystal ball started to smoke!

"I see danger!" she said. "You will meet your doom if you stay in these mountains!"

"What does it say about Franken Castle?" asked Velma. "That's where we're heading!"

"The caretaker ran away in fear today!" Carlotta shrieked. "Stay away or face your doom!"

Back in the van, the gang headed onward. Lightning cracked around the creepy castle. The moon was full! "What a pad for ghosts!" said Shaggy. "Hello? Anybody home?"

The gang got out and walked around. The drawbridge suddenly dropped open with a mighty clang! "Let's cross!" said Freddy.

But halfway across the bridge, a vampire ghost suddenly appeared! "Stop! You're not welcome here!" he shouted. "Go *now*, or abandon all hope of seeing the sun rise again!"

Suddenly, a vampire bat flew toward them! The gang ran to escape when the drawbridge started to rise! Daphne didn't make it! She was stuck hanging from the raised bridge! She tumbled down in front of the castle, at the feet of a green Frankenstein monster! "Run, Daphne! Run!" yelled Velma.

"Don't worry! I'm running!" she replied.

"Shaggy! We've got to get across that moat!" said a worried Freddy. "He's after Daphne!"

Freddy lassoed a castle statue above the door. Shaggy swung over the moat, with Scooby hanging on for dear life! "Scooby-Dooby-Doo!!" he screamed. They plopped on the other side and lowered the drawbridge, barely missing an alligator in the castle's moat!

Inside the castle, Shaggy heard a growl behind him! "Quit clowning around, Scooby!" he said. Then he turned and looked! "A werewolf!!" Shaggy screamed. "Scooby-Doo, where are you??" Shaggy and Scooby ran as fast as they could!

Scooby hid in a piano until the werewolf smashed it into a million pieces! Then, with piano keys for teeth, a quick-thinking Scooby stood on his hind legs, acted like a vicious monster, and scared the werewolf away!

"Good boy, Scooby!" said a grateful Shaggy.

In another part of the castle, Freddy and Velma continued to look for Daphne. "First Daphne disappears, now Shaggy and Scooby, too!" said a worried Velma. "Where could they be?"

Above them, the vampire ghost reappeared in a cloud of smoke and screamed his warning. "You'll never leave this castle now!" Then a bat swooped down at them!

"Duck, Velma!" yelled Freddy.

Crawling to safety, Velma hit her head on a table, causing her glasses to fly across the room! "My glasses!" cried Velma. "I can't see without them!" She crawled across the room toward a roaring fireplace! She was about to touch the hot flame when the wall opened up and swallowed Velma behind it!

"Coast is clear, Scooby," Shaggy said as they stumbled into a kitchen. "I think we gave ol' fuzzy face the slip! Hey, look! A refrig!"

Scooby checked out the refrigerator. "Raggy! Rome Rere!" he barked.

Shaggy read the labels from the jars on the shelf: "Pickled Vampire Wings! Yuk! Werewolf snacks! Fried Moonbeams! Double Yuk Yuk! What a menu!"

Just then, Frankenstein's monster reappeared! Scooby and Shaggy made a quick exit, and ran into Velma! She'd wandered into a torchure chamber! Luckily, Shaggy had an extra pair of Velma's glasses!

From far off they heard a cry. "Help! Help me!" They peeked down through iron bars in an opening on the dusty floor. There was Daphne at the bottom of the pit! Shaggy dropped a rope for Daphne and pulled her up.

Scooby, Shaggy, Velma and Daphne followed through a dark tunnel. At the other end they found Freddy.

"Hey gang, I think I found a clue in that pit!" said Daphne. "A message on the wall, written in 1668: *I have fooled them all! I may perish, but I'll be as rich as King Tut!*"

"King Tut was an Egyptian who had his riches buried with him in his crypt," Velma explained. "I'll bet the treasure is buried in the Franken Family crypt! Let's go!"

Poor Scooby didn't want to go! On the other hand, he didn't exactly want to stay behind by himself, either! "Rait for re!" he barked.

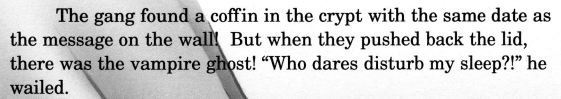

The gang found a coffin in the crypt with the same date as the message on the wall! But when they pushed back the lid, there was the vampire ghost! "Who dares disturb my sleep?!" he wailed.

"Every man for himself!" Shaggy yelled, as everybody took off! The vampire was close behind.

Scooby pulled a tapestry off the wall to try and catch the vampire ghost.

The ghost kept running! He ran right into the tapestry held high by Scooby and Shaggy! But the trap didn't work! With the tapestry wrapped around him, he jumped back into the coffin!

"Come on, gang!" yelled Freddy. "We've got him trapped!"
But when they opened the coffin, it was empty! They found only a
ruby, a diamond and a gold earring. Some pearls were sewn onto
a piece of tapestry. "Hmmm," said Freddy. "I've seen this earring
somewhere before!"

"That's what the clue meant!" said Velma. "The Franken
Family jewels were sewn into the tapestry!"

"But the ghost took it away!" said Daphne.

"That was no ghost!" said Freddy. "I think we'll pay that
gypsy another visit!"

The gang returned to the gypsy's wagon. "What a surprise to see you again, my pretties!" she said. "How was your visit to the castle?"

"We might ask you the same question," Freddy said.

"Me? I never go to the castle!"

In came Scooby, pulling the tapestry from behind the gypsy. "Give me that, you mutt!" screamed the gypsy in a much deeper voice! Grabbing the tapestry, the gypsy ran from the wagon!

"Get him, Scooby!" yelled Velma, as she ran after the gypsy. They played tug-o-war with the jeweled tapestry until a police car pulled up.

"The caretaker called and said there was trouble at the castle," said the sheriff. The gypsy's disguise had fallen off. "Why, it's Big Bob Oakley, alias 'The Actor', a master of disguise!" the sheriff exclaimed. "He's wanted in seven states!"

"He's been haunting the castle to scare people away!" exclaimed Freddy.

"He was after the Franken Family jewels!" said Daphne.

"Yes, and I would have gotten away with it, too! If it wasn't for those blasted kids and their dog!" sighed Big Bob.

The sheriff took Big Bob away and thanked the gang for their good work. So the gang settled into a picnic, with a huge stack of Shaggy's sandwiches. Just as Shaggy started to take a bite, a bat headed right for them! "Save my sandwich!" yelled Shaggy.

"Look!" said Freddy. "It was just a stuffed bat on a wire!"

Down the wire came someone else! Chomp!

"Huh?" said Shaggy, as he watched Scooby fly off with the stack of sandwiches. "Hey Scooby! I always knew you were a little batty!"

Scooby just giggled and barked, "Scooby-Dooby-Doooo!"